Amos Gets Famous

Gary Paulsen

Amos Gets Famous

CULPEPPER
ADVENTURES

A YEARLING BOOK

Published by
Dell Publishing
a division of
Bantam Doubleday Dell Publishing Group, Inc.
666 Fifth Avenue
New York, New York 10103

ISBN: 0-440-40749-4

Printed in the United States of America

January 1993

10 9 8 7 6 5 4 3 2 1

OPM

Amos Gets Famous

Chapter · 1

Duncan—Dunc—Culpepper and Amos Binder were riding their mountain bikes through the woods on the way to the library.

"What a great day," Dunc said. "You don't get many Saturdays like this."

"Don't try to talk me out of it." Amos Binder pumped away right behind him.

"I wasn't going to. I like the library." The problem was, Dunc didn't know if he liked it enough to spend a beautiful afternoon there. It was a sacrifice. He had to make those every once in a while for Amos. Amos was his best friend for life.

"I sure hope she's there." Amos was in love

with a girl named Melissa Hansen and had been ever since he got out of diapers, or so it seemed. Despite the fact that Melissa had done mouth-to-mouth resuscitation on Amos when he nearly drowned and hugged him when he had turned into a dog and even spoken to him when she thought he was his own cousin, she really didn't even know his name. That didn't stop Amos.

"Why did you say we're doing this?" Dunc asked.

"Because I saw Melissa doing her homework there once."

"Once." Dunc accelerated into a gully and downshifted to come up the other side.

"I know—it was two months ago. But if she was there once, she'll be there again."

Dunc sighed. They whipped around a basswood tree. They were deep in the woods now, so deep they couldn't even hear the city traffic.

"She called me yesterday," Amos said.

"Did she?"

"Yeah, well . . . kind of."

"What do you mean?"

"I was out mowing the lawn. I was just fin-

2

ishing up the B in my initials—I always mow my initials in the lawn first—when I heard the phone ring. It was Melissa's ring."

"Oh." Dunc nodded his head. Amos swore up and down that Melissa's ring was different from everybody else's.

"I headed for the living room as fast as I could go," Amos said. "Things were going perfectly—I mean good form, legs pumping right. I made the phone before the second ring, and I was thinking, all right, I've got it this time."

"What happened?"

"I remembered."

"Remembered what?"

"That I was still pushing the lawn mower. I ran over the telephone cord. When I picked up the receiver, it was dead."

"Too bad. Watch your head." Dunc ducked. So did Amos.

"Luckily, no one was home," Amos continued. "I pulled the mower back outside and ran down to the hardware store to buy a new cord. Of course, Mom and Dad found out what had happened anyway."

"How?"

3

"We have that nice shag carpeting in the living room. Or used to. Boy, was Dad mad." Amos upshifted to pick up speed. He flew off the top of a little knoll and didn't land until he reached the bottom. He loved doing that.

"Did you hear about the burglary ring?" Amos also liked to talk while mountain biking. Dunc liked to pay attention to what he was doing. That's why Dunc always came out of the woods without a scratch, while Amos always resembled a television commercial for Band-Aids.

"They struck again," he said.

"Yeah?"

"That makes seven robberies in seven days."

Dunc slowed down for a second to let a chipmunk pass. "What did they steal this time?"

"An antique gold nosering."

"I guess that's no big surprise." So far, the burglars had stolen an old portrait, three spoons, a washtub, and various other odds and ends. At first glance it would seem that none of it was worth much, but first glances aren't always right. The washtub originally belonged to Napoleon and was worth close to half a million dollars.

4

"Are there any clues?" Dunc asked.

"Not for sure—there's a maybe clue in the paper. I'll show it to you when we get to the library."

Dunc powered up a hill and stopped on its summit. He waited. Amos stopped beside him. They looked down.

Below them lay Ghastly Gulch. At the bottom flowed Suicide Stream. Together they had claimed more than one inexperienced biker. It had taken Dunc three runs before he figured out how to cross it. Amos had tried a hundred times and still hadn't figured it out.

"You know what to do, right?" Dunc asked.

"Right. Hang on, close my eyes, and pray."

"No. Gun it as fast as you can until you get to the big oak tree, then veer to the right to avoid the root. Swing back to the left, or you'll hit the rocks in the stream. Got it?"

"Got it—"

Dunc started down.

"—I think." Amos followed him. *Just do what Dunc does,* he said to himself.

Dunc hunched forward. So did Amos. Dunc swerved right when he reached the oak tree. So

5

did Amos. Dunc ducked under a low branch of a maple tree.

Amos didn't.

He ducked too soon. When he straightened up again he hadn't cleared the branch.

It wasn't a pretty sight.

His arms flew up for protection. He managed to get by the branch with only a few leaves and twigs hitting his face. But since his hands were off the handlebars, when he was supposed to turn left, he couldn't. His front tire hit a rock, and the bike flew up in the air.

When Dunc reached the top on the other side he looked back. Amos's bike was coming up the hill by itself.

Amos was kissing a tree.

"Quit fooling around, Amos."

Amos peeled his face off. The imprint of the bark was driven into his cheeks.

"Are you all right?"

Amos nodded. "I'm getting better." He pulled a maple leaf out of his left nostril.

"What do you mean?"

"I didn't almost kill myself until *after* the oak tree. That's the best I've ever done. Next time, I won't almost kill myself until after the stream."

He grabbed his bike as it rolled back toward him and ran up the hill.

"Let's get going," he said. "Melissa might be there right now."

Chapter · 2

"I'm bored, Dunc." Amos folded up the newspaper and set it on the table.

"This was your idea." Dunc studied his book.

"I know, but it's almost five o'clock." He sighed. "I don't think she's going to show. Let's go."

"Not now. I'm interested in this."

"I don't have anything to do."

"Finish the newspaper."

"I already read all the important parts."

Dunc looked up. "Like what?"

"The funnies and the sports page."

"Those are the important parts?"

"Sure. In the Foofy the Dog strip, Foofy tried to get the dog food out of the cupboard, and—"

"Why don't you read the front page? Find out what's happening in the world."

"I already know—nothing. Melissa didn't show up."

"I'm not leaving until I finish this chapter. Here—read the newspaper article about the burglary ring."

"All right." Amos picked the paper back up. "Here's that clue I told you about. It's an ad in the Personals column with yesterday's date and the numbers fifteen, four, and twenty, the letter P, the word *ring,* and the name *Mr. Zipzoo* on it. The police think it might be a clue—that's what it said in the article anyway."

"It doesn't make much sense, does it?" Dunc looked up.

"What about Mr. Zipzoo?"

"Maybe he's the ringleader."

"Must be."

Dunc concentrated on his book again.

"What are you reading?" Amos asked.

"It's a book about parasitic nematodes."

"Parasitic nema-what?"

"Todes. Nematodes. Roundworms."

9

Amos wrinkled up his face. "That's gross. Why would you want to read a book like that?"

"It's fascinating. Most of them are microscopic, but the Guinea roundworm can grow to over three feet long. Look, here's a picture of it."

"I don't want to see it."

"Come on, Amos—it's cool." He flipped the book across the table. As he did, a slip of paper fell out of it and fluttered to the floor.

"What's that?" Amos asked.

"It's the roundworm," Dunc said, pointing to the picture. "You can actually see it wriggling under this guy's skin."

"Not the picture," Amos said. "The paper. A piece of paper fell out of the book."

Dunc reached down and picked it up. He looked at both sides and shook his head. "Weird."

"What?"

"It has a date, an address, the word *clock,* and—" He stopped.

"And what?" said Amos.

"What did you say the name on the note the police found was?"

"Mr. Zipzoo."

"That's on here too," Dunc said.

Amos stared at him. "Do you think—"

"I don't know. Could be. Think we should check it out?"

Amos leaned back in his chair and shook his head. He looked across the table as if Dunc had some kind of skin disease. "Whenever we check something out, something bad happens."

"That's not true."

"Sure it is. Either parrots swear at me, or ghosts scare me so bad I pee my pants, or dogs blow snot all over me. We have bad luck."

"You have bad luck."

"Same difference." He turned the page in the book so he wouldn't have to look at the round-worm.

"You'll do fine this time," Dunc said.

"How do you know that?"

"Because you've had bad luck all your life. How long do you think a streak like that can last?" Dunc looked back down at the note. "I wonder what those numbers in the paper meant."

"What were they, again?" Amos asked.

"Fifteen, four, twenty, and there's a P at the end."

"I don't know." A thoughtful look crawled

like a bug across Amos's face. "Maybe Mr. Zipzoo is an alien, and he's collecting knick-knacks from Earth for a museum on his home planet. Maybe the numbers are spatial coordinates, like they use on TV. Spatial coordinates always sound like that."

Dunc ignored him. "I bet this is a message from Mr. Zipzoo to one of the burglars that works for him. There's one thing I don't understand—why would he leave messages in library books? Anybody could find them."

"No way. How many people are strange enough to look in a book about parasitic nematodes?"

"I did."

Amos nodded. "My point exactly. I bet that book has been sitting on the shelf for years without ever being opened. When was the last time someone checked it out?"

Dunc flipped to the back cover. "Nineteen fifty-three."

"See what I mean? What safer place could there be to hide a note?"

"Except now we found it. We know the place, the date, and what they're going to steal," said Dunc.

"Maybe we should go to the police."

Dunc shook his head. "Don't you remember the appliance smugglers?"

"Oh, yeah. I guess we can't go to the police." Dunc and Amos had once found an underground tunnel that some appliance thieves were using for storage. It was filled with gunpowder barrels from the Civil War. One of the thieves had lit a match and taken out most of that side of town. The police were still a little touchy about it.

"This address looks familiar," Dunc said. "Do you know it?" He handed the paper to Amos.

Amos read it. His head popped up.

"What?" Dunc asked.

"That," Amos almost shouted, "is Melissa's address!"

Chapter·3

"Think about it, Dunc. We can be heroes!"

Dunc shook his head. "I don't want to be a hero."

"Not just a hero," Amos said. "I'll be *a hero*. I'll rush into Melissa's house and save her from some big dastardly brute. She'll love me forever."

"Speaking of big dastardly brutes, I saw in the paper that her brother Rocko is home from college. What happens if he catches us in his house?"

"Big deal."

"Maybe you forgot. He plays the offensive line for one of those Big Ten football teams."

"What position?"

"I didn't say he plays a position. I said he plays the line. The whole line."

"So? If we catch this burglar and save Melissa and her family, Rocko will be my friend for life. A guy like that is good to have for a friend."

Dunc slid the paper back into the book and put it on the shelf. He turned and studied his friend and thought, *Right there is the problem. He is my friend. My best friend for life. And here is a chance for him to realize his dream.* He sighed. Amos's dream was to get to talk to Melissa. He knew he had to do this thing—for Amos. *But it would hurt,* he thought. Somehow he would hurt himself.

Amos had been going on all this time. "They'll be so grateful in that house, they'll probably ask me to move in. I can see it now. Melissa will think the sun rises and sets on me—"

Dunc stopped him. A small figure, not more than five feet tall, walked into the aisle past Dunc. He put his face up close to the row of books at the beginning of the aisle and started moving sideways down the aisle, staring at each book as he moved. Then he stopped, reached up, and took the nematode book down. He opened it, put the note into his pocket, and hurried past Dunc and Amos and out of the library. He was wearing a hat pulled low and a jacket with the collar up, so it was impossible to see his face.

Amos watched him leave. "I wonder . . ."

"Wonder what?" Dunc was moving toward the door.

"I wonder if the clock he's going to steal is in Melissa's room."

Dunc shook his head. "Man, you're hopeless. Come on, we've got to follow that guy."

Dunc made for the door with Amos following, but outside there was no sign of the man. The streets were empty except for some girls and boys crossing at the corner. There was a row of maples with thick foliage along the street, and Dunc thought he heard a sound up in the trees but could see nothing and shook his head. "I don't know how, but he's gone, just gone."

"Maybe he's faster than we thought."

"Must be." Dunc started down the steps. "Let's get home."

"Home? Why? It's still early."

"We have to get some rest."

"Rest?"

"So we can be alert tonight when we try to catch this guy."

"Ah—I almost forgot."

Amos followed him down the sidewalk.

Chapter · 4

The moon was full that night. It lit up the Hansen yard silver, almost as bright as day.

"Keep your eyes peeled," Dunc whispered. He and Amos lay together in the bushes by the front walk.

"Peeling my eyes—what a stupid expression. Can I do that like an orange, or do I need a knife?"

"Quiet!" Dunc pointed. A shadow darted through the trees at the side of the house.

Amos shook his head. "It's a dog." Ever since the time he'd been bitten by a werewolf and turned into a dog, Amos thought everything was a dog.

Dunc shook his head. "Since when do dogs walk on two legs?" He pointed again. The shadow melted into a shrub next to the house. It was the small burglar.

"How's he going to get in?" Amos whispered. "He's too short to reach the window."

As if in answer to his question, the man jumped. He caught the second-story windowsill above his head with one hand and silently opened the window with the other while he was hanging there. One swing of his legs, and he was inside.

"Did you see that?" Amos asked.

"Yeah."

"No, I mean did you *see* that? That little guy could slam-dunk a basketball."

"Let's go." Dunc slunk toward the house. Amos followed him until they stood beneath the open window.

Amos jumped, but he couldn't get close to reaching the sill. "Now what do we do?"

Dunc studied the window. "I'll have to stand on your shoulders."

"What do you mean, stand on my shoulders? Why can't I stand on yours?"

"If I stand on your shoulders, I should be

able to reach the sill. If you stand on mine, you probably won't. You're shorter than I am."

Amos looked into Dunc's eyes. "That's crazy."

But Dunc was already pushing Amos into position. "Come on, give me a boost." Amos shook his head, but he bent and cupped his hands. Dunc heaved himself up and put one foot on Amos's shoulder, then the second.

It wasn't quite enough. "If I can just get a little more height—"

"You just stuck your toe in my eye."

"Move a little to the left. I can reach the shutter but not the sill next to it."

Amos moved.

"Just let me get a little closer." Dunc stepped on the top of Amos's head. His fingers gripped the edge of the sill. "Made it."

He bounced once on Amos's head for momentum, then scrabbled his feet on the siding and up through the window. Then he reached down to help Amos up.

Amos didn't look happy. "Man, it's going to take a week to get my hair clean again."

"At least we're in, aren't we?" Dunc took a flashlight out of his pocket. He flashed it once, then shut it off again.

20

"Did you see a clock?" he asked.

"No."

"I didn't either. There's a desk, a chair, a standing lamp, and a bookcase. This must be Mr. Hansen's study."

"Did you see the little guy?"

"No."

"Then he must be somewhere else. Let's check Melissa's room first." They tiptoed across the floor.

Just as Dunc reached for the knob, the door slowly began to open. The small man walked in, carrying a clock tucked under his arm.

Chapter · 5

The man wore a black body suit, a face mask, and gloves. He dropped into a half-crouch, which made him seem about half as tall as the boys, and gave a low growl.

Amos stuck his chest out and pushed Dunc to the side. "Melissa's my girlfriend," he said. "Let me be the hero." He tried to grab the clock.

Later Amos could not remember exactly what happened. He remembered touching the clock and the small man grabbing his wrist. He remembered looking at his feet and seeing the ceiling, walls, bathroom door, ceiling, walls, and bathroom door, and then a doorknob seemed to fly at him and hit him exactly in the middle of his forehead. After that things became hazy.

When he came to, he was outside the study propped up against the wall, standing on his head. His face was mashed into the angle the wall made with the floor and his left hand and foot waved crazily at each other.

"Try to be quiet," Dunc whispered to him, seeing that he was conscious again.

Amos fell over, climbed slowly to his feet, and shook his head.

"Be quiet?" Amos said. "I'm tossed through the air like a beach ball, and you tell me to be quiet. Fine. Next time I'll crash into the wall silently."

Dunc stood in front of the window of the study, his arms spread like a goalie trying to guard a net. The burglar was darting back and forth in front of him, dodging left and right. The clock was still under his arm. He was trying to slip by Dunc to get to the window.

"Amos," Dunc hissed, "help me!"

"On my way."

Amos charged back into the room—or tried to charge. His shoes had come untied in the cartwheeling, and his feet now became hopelessly tangled in the laces. He just had time to think how much like a phone call this was all turning out to be as he sailed over the burglar, over Dunc's shoulder, and out the window.

At the last possible half second his hand caught the sill, and instead of flying clear through the window, his body straightened and described a perfect arc. He slammed backfirst against the outside of the house. He hit so hard, the snot flew out of his nose. He hung for a second by the one hand. Then his fingers loosened, and he dropped like a sack of garbage into the flower beds next to the wall.

"Here, grab on." Dunc leaned quickly out the window. "I'll pull you back in."

Amos stood, grabbed Dunc's hand, and jumped as Dunc pulled. Amos flew back into the window and hit the burglar, who was still trying to get past Dunc to the window.

Amos and the burglar went down in a heap, flopped, came up, crashed into a desk, took a floor lamp over, and broke a chair with a sound like a full-scale war, before coming to their feet.

For part of a second everything stopped. The burglar stared at Amos and Dunc, while they stared at him. Then the burglar looked up at the ceiling.

Footsteps.

All the noise had awakened somebody.

The burglar snarled one more time, and before Dunc could stop him, he dived over his shoulder out into the darkness with the clock under his arm, and he was gone.

Just like that. Gone.

"Oh, man." Broken splinters from the chair were stuck in Amos's shirt. He looked like a porcupine. "Where'd he go?"

"Forget him. Let's get out of here."

"Why did you let him get away?"

Dunc's mouth dropped open. "Why did *I* let him get away? What were you doing all this time?"

"All right, if you want to argue, let's argue. I—"

"There's no time for that now. We have to get out of here." The footsteps came downstairs. Dunc climbed out the window and dropped to the ground. Amos followed him.

As he hung from the windowsill, Amos saw a light come on in the study. A man the size of a small herd of buffalo squeezed through the door.

His shoulders popped against the doorframe like a cork pulled from a bottle.

Rocko.

"What happens here?" Rocko had mastered football but not the English language.

Amos didn't stick around to answer him. He let go and landed in the flowers beneath the window. He and Dunc ran for the trees on the far side of the yard.

Just before they disappeared into the darkness, Amos looked back over his shoulder. Melissa was leaning over the window and looking straight at him.

It's like Romeo and Juliet, he thought. *And there she is, leaning over the balcony. I should say something poetic, something from Shakespeare about saving her life, and—*

Because he was looking back at Melissa, he didn't see the rake that was lying near the front shrubbery with the tines pointed up. He stepped perfectly on them, and the rake handle whipped up and smashed him directly in the center of his face.

What he said was in no way connected with Shakespeare.

Chapter · 6

Amos was famous.

Or something like Amos was close to famous.

Melissa had gotten a fair look at him in the partial light from the streetlight, but she didn't know it was Amos.

She thought he was the burglar.

And she had worked with the police artist and his Identi-Kit to come up with a picture of the supposed burglar, which now covered the top half of the front page of the paper under the headline:

HAVE YOU SEEN THIS FACE?

27

The story beneath the picture told anybody who has seen the face to tell the police, for a reward.

Three things saved Amos. First, Melissa hadn't seen him very well, and the picture barely matched Amos's face—although there was something about the eyes, something about the corners of the eyes, that seemed to show something of Amos. The second thing that saved Amos was the rake handle. It had caught him slap across the middle of his face and had done a lot to temporarily rearrange his looks. The third thing was that Amos had fallen into the dirt and flowers below the windowsill, and his upper lip and the sides of his face had been smeared either with dirt or fertilizer—he hoped dirt.

The picture in the paper had a moustache and sideburns.

"We have to go back," Dunc said.

"Back where?" Amos was massaging his nose where the rake handle had caught him. It looked like a ripe plum. An overripe plum. They were sitting in Dunc's room, where everything was neat and organized—unlike Amos's room, where it was impossible to sit because every-

28

thing *wasn't* neat and organized. They had the newspaper spread on the bed next to them, the front-page picture looking up at Amos.

"Back to Melissa's house," Dunc said. "We have to make the burglar come back there and catch him there to clear your name."

Amos shook his head. "Nobody will recognize me from that picture. I'd be the only boy in middle school with a dark moustache and sideburns if I looked like that."

"Just the same—it's an ax hanging over your head." Dunc pointed at the picture. "It will follow you the rest of your life—it might wind up *ruining* your life."

"The rake almost ruined my life, and the burglar throwing me around almost ruined my life, and trying to learn to fly when I went through the window almost ruined my life, and slamming into the wall almost ruined my life." Amos pointed to the paper. "That picture isn't going to ruin my life."

"Melissa."

Amos stopped. "What?"

"You have to go back because of Melissa—she needs you."

29

Amos sighed. "Dunc, she's the one who turned me in to the police."

"She didn't know it was you. She needs you to catch this guy and get the reward and be a hero."

"You're nuts."

But his voice had weakened, and Dunc knew he had him.

"The way I see it," Dunc said, pushing the paper aside, "is we have to draw the burglar out."

"How are we going to do that? He's holed up somewhere by now."

"Maybe. Maybe not. It depends on how greedy Mr. Zipzoo is. He's the one giving the orders."

"So what do we do?"

"How does Mr. Zipzoo communicate with the burglar?" Dunc asked.

"Through notes at the library."

"Right. So if we leave a note . . ."

"So all we have to do is put a note in the nematode book telling the burglar to steal something from the Hansens tonight, right?"

"Wrong."

"What do you mean, wrong?"

"The next note doesn't go in the nematode book. That's what the numbers are for. They direct the burglar to the new book's location."

"How?"

"I don't know yet."

"So the plan is to put a note in the right book telling the burglar to steal something from the Hansens after dark tonight. Now do I have it?"

"Sort of. He can't steal just anything. It has to be something that will take him a while to steal."

"Like what?"

"I've been thinking about that. I think we'll have him steal the toilet bowl out of the bathroom."

Amos stared at him. "The toilet bowl?"

"Sure. It'll take him a long time to shut the water off and get the bowl up off the floor. Once he does, he won't be able to run very fast because it's so heavy."

"Good thinking." Amos nodded. "Better yet, how about the refrigerator or the front steps? Or the whole house?"

"Amos . . ."

"Well, come on, Dunc. This is nuts—stealing toilets. You're crazy."

"No, it'll work. Trust me."

"Don't say that—don't say 'trust me.' The last time you said that, I wound up getting turned into a dog and had to fight my way out of a nest of pit bulls, and before that a parrot swore at me, and—"

"Not this time. I promise." Dunc stood up. "Come on, let's head down to the library and work on these codes."

They were halfway to the door when Dunc stopped and turned. "You'd better wear a disguise."

"Why? Nobody will know me from that picture."

"It's there, in the eyes—it looks like you there. Why don't you wear sunglasses?"

They tore the house apart and finally found a pair of sunglasses. Unfortunately, they belonged to Dunc's little sister. They were pink with false molded plastic lashes that went up at the corners and had little flowers painted on the rims.

"No," Amos said. "I'd rather go to prison."

But Dunc explained that his eyes would give him away and that he wouldn't be able to become a hero in jail and that nobody would know it was him and that they were on the third planet from the Sun and that the vernal equinox was due any day and that for every action there was an equal and opposite reaction and that all these things factored into the tangent of the two lines . . .

Amos wore the glasses.

Chapter·7

Dunc opened the door of the library.

Inside, people were huddled over books and newspapers. Dunc moved to the newspapers, looked through the ads, and found one with the same type of numbers. "Here it is—the code. Thirty, five, sixty-three, and the letter E."

"That doesn't mean anything to me." Amos looked around the library and shook his head, the glasses flashing in the light.

"We have to figure out what the numbers on the note mean," Dunc said. "Using the other set. What were they again?"

"The numbers out of the paper the last time

were fifteen, four, twenty, and the letter was P. Which doesn't mean anything."

"I was up half the night thinking about that. It might be the Dewey Decimal code for a book, only split up."

"You mean like 154.20?"

"Yeah. Let's go check it out."

They hurried back toward the aisles.

"This could be kind of fun," Amos said.

Dunc ignored him. "Here's the one hundreds. Follow me."

A moment later Amos stopped. "You're wrong, Dunc."

"Why do you say that?"

"Because here's 154.20. It's a book about achieving higher consciousness."

"Hm." Dunc tapped his chin. He thought hard.

"Don't overdo it, Dunc."

"Leave me alone."

"There's smoke coming out of your ears."

"If you don't let me think, I'm not going to be able to help you. You'll be on the run the rest of your life."

"All right, I'm sorry. Go ahead and think. Can't even take a joke."

Dunc snapped his fingers. "I have it!"

"Have what?"

"Follow me." Dunc led Amos back toward the newspaper section. He stopped at the first bookshelf.

"What was the first number?"

"Fifteen."

"Start counting bookshelves." Amos followed Dunc as he strode away from the newspapers. He stopped at shelf number fifteen.

"What was the second number?"

"Four." Dunc counted down four shelves from the top.

"What was the third number?"

"Twenty." Dunc counted books in from the end of the shelf. When he reached the twentieth book, he stopped and sighed.

"What's the book?"

"*All About Bears*. I'm wrong." He collapsed back against the shelf behind him. "How could that be? It just isn't possible." It was hard on Dunc to be wrong, and he chewed his lower lip. *Someday,* Amos thought, *he'll chew that lip off.*

"I guess we'll have to find some way of smuggling you out of the city," Dunc said.

"Dunc . . ."

"Maybe we can find a cabin up north in the woods you can hide in. You'll have to snare rabbits for food. Do you know how to snare?"

"Dunc . . ."

"It doesn't matter. The police will catch us before we get there anyway."

"Dunc, if you were a very small man, wouldn't you start counting at the bottom shelf?"

Dunc smiled. "Could it be—" They hurried to the end of the aisle and started over.

"We're still wrong," Dunc said. "Twenty books in is *The Wonderful World of Leeches*."

"But we're close. *Parasitic Nematodes* is only three more books."

"It's not close enough. If we put the fake note in the wrong book, we're no better off than we were when we started."

"I suppose it's impossible to be accurate with people checking books out and the librarian reshelving them all the time." Amos scratched his head. "Wait a minute. What about the letter?"

"The letter?"

"The P." Amos snapped his fingers. "I got it. Mr. Zipzoo put that on the end in case the num-

37

bers didn't come out quite right. P—*Parasitic Nematodes*. Get it?"

Dunc smiled again. "Why are you so smart today?"

"It must be the pressure of being a fugitive from justice." Amos took the glasses off for a moment, but a man reading the paper, looking at the front page, seemed to stare at him for too long, and he put them back on. "Let's find the book for the next burglary."

Thirty aisles in, five rows up, sixty-three books from the end. Dunc stopped and stared at Amos.

"What?" Amos asked.

"The book's called *Early French Erotica of the Nineteen Thirties*."

Amos's mouth dropped open. "Erotica? Does that mean dirty stories?"

"That's exactly what it means."

"My mom and dad would kill me if they knew I looked at a book like that."

"Mine too," Dunc said.

They stared at the book.

"Still," Amos said, "it's for a good cause."

Dunc nodded. "It's not as if we'd normally

38

look at a book like this. We have to. I certainly don't *want* to."

"Me either."

"Right. Let me see it." They both reached at the same time.

"I grabbed it first, Dunc. Let go."

"No, you didn't. I did. You can see it after I'm done. I—"

Dunc stopped in midsentence. His hands dropped to his sides. A policeman had just stepped into the aisle behind Amos and was staring at them.

Chapter · 8

"I knew you'd see it my way," Amos said.

Dunc didn't say anything.

"I just want to see if there are any pictures. After that you can have it."

Dunc still didn't say anything.

"Rats, no pictures. What kind of a book is this? Do you think we have time to read some before the burglar gets here?"

"Burglar?" A deep voice came from behind Amos's shoulder, and he turned and dropped the book. "Did you say something about a burglar?" The policeman picked the book up and handed it to Amos. He didn't look at the cover.

"Thank you," Amos answered. His voice

squeaked. He looked at the policeman's name tag. OFFICER CLARK.

"Your voice changed," said the policeman.

"Did it? I mean, it did."

"He has a cold," Dunc said.

"Yes, that's it," Amos said. "I have a cold. The school is so drafty." He coughed and held the book behind his back.

"What's this about a burglar?"

"Oh, nothing. We're just talking about all the burglaries that have been going on." Dunc shrugged. "You know, just talking. Kind of just —talking. About the burglaries. Talking."

"What's the book you're reading?" The policeman asked.

"What book?"

"The one behind your back."

Amos took the book out. "This? Uh . . . uh—"

Officer Clark glanced at the cover. He eyed Amos suspiciously. "What are two young boys doing reading a book like this?"

Amos said nothing. He suddenly realized that he was wearing a pair of pink sunglasses with flowers on them and holding a dirty book and looking up at a policeman and that he was a fugitive from justice, except that he thought of it as a FUGITIVE FROM JUSTICE, all in capitals, and his tongue had stuck to the roof of his mouth as if it were covered with Superglue.

"It's research," Dunc interrupted. "We have to do a paper on the evils of the world."

"Yes. All the evil, so much evil." Amos found his voice. "Lots of it out there, evil. Just about waist deep, evil. I never saw so much evil."

Dunc pinched him, and he shut up. The policeman eyed them both suspiciously, but after what seemed like hours to the boys, he handed the book back to Amos. "You'd better put the book back and move on to another aisle, don't you think?"

Amos and Dunc both nodded. They were still nodding while Officer Clark turned and left them standing there.

"That was close," Dunc said. He took the book down, opened it, took out a piece of paper, and put his own piece of paper inside.

"What's that?" Amos asked.

"Instructions telling the burglar to go to Melissa's house and steal a toilet. Let's go."

"Already?"

"The burglar could be here any minute."

42

"We have a few minutes, don't we? I'd kind of like to look at that book."

"There's no time. Let's go."

On their way out, they passed the same short, roundly built man with long arms and coat and hat they had seen the first time. Dunc had his face behind Amos, and Amos had turned to say something, so they didn't see him. The short man didn't see their faces clearly, but he heard their voices, and he turned and watched their backs as they moved down the library steps and onto the sidewalk.

Then he made his way into the library and to the shelf with the book about early French erotica.

Chapter · 9

"So tell me the plan again," Amos whispered. They were in the bushes near Melissa's house. It was dark, and they had been waiting for over two hours—long enough for Amos to lose his patience.

"You already know it."

"I just want to be sure."

"This is the last time," Dunc said. "We hide here until the burglar goes inside. I run and call the police. The police arrive, and we tell them the reason we're here is that we're trying to warn Melissa. The burglar is arrested, and your name is cleared. Simple."

"I hate that word."

"What word?"

"*Simple.* You use it with everything, but nothing ever turns out to be that way."

"Amos—"

"I hate it, too, when you say my name that way. 'Amos.' As if you're talking to a lamp pole. You always say *simple* and it isn't, and you say *Amos* when you really don't expect . . ." He trailed off and turned.

In back of them, in the bushes, there was a rustling sound, and a small figure with long arms appeared. It walked with a rolling gait across the lawn and stopped below a different second-story window from the last time. With an easy jump the figure leaped up to hang from the windowsill by one arm. He used the other arm to reach up and open the window. Then easily he swung up and into the house.

"The burglar," Dunc whispered. "He's in."

"Dunc . . ."

"I'll go call the police."

"Dunc . . ."

"You keep watch, and I'll be right back."

"Dunc . . ."

"What?"

45

"That's Melissa's room. The one he climbed into. That's her room."

"How do you know that?"

"Because I come by here sometimes. Well, lots of times. It's only twelve blocks out of my way in the opposite direction on the way to school, and I know it's her room because I've seen her in the window. It's about a hundred and thirty-six point four feet from the street to her room."

Dunc stared at him. " 'About'?"

"Well, exactly. I used a tape measure one time when they were on vacation."

Dunc shook his head. "That doesn't change anything. He's still in there, and I still have to run for the police."

"No. There's no time for the police. We have to get in there and save her."

Amos turned to run for the house and promptly stepped on the rake, which was lying in exactly the same place that it had been lying last time. The handle came up as it had before, perfectly, and caught him vertically exactly between the eyes. The damage might not have been so bad except that he was still wearing the pink sunglasses and the glasses were driven solidly into his forehead, while the side pieces slammed back and into his temples. It was about like having a vise close instantly on his head, and he stopped dead, his mind blown completely blank.

Dunc moved around him. "Come on, Amos. You're right. Let's get in there."

Amos nodded. "In there."

Dunc stopped next to the wall below the window.

Amos walked toward him, a half-smile on his face.

"Come *on*." Dunc grabbed him and jerked him up against the wall, turned him to face outward, climbed up his front side by stepping in on Amos's belt, which pulled his pants halfway down, then on his shoulders and head and up to grab the sill. Amos stood smiling peacefully the whole time.

Dunc clambered into the window, reached back and down, and caught Amos by the back of his T-shirt. With a heave he pulled Amos up backward into the room. Amos stood in the darkened room, smiling quietly to himself, his pants around his knees.

47

Melissa slept quietly not six feet from him. Amos had no idea she was there.

He had no ideas at all. The inside of his mind was totally blank.

Chapter · 10

Time has a way of being elastic. Candy goes like lightning, and a math test can take a whole lifetime, and the time that Amos stood smiling in Melissa's room could have been two minutes or two weeks. It didn't matter.

Amos was unconscious.

His eyes were open, but they didn't focus. They stared out and out and out, and he was smiling, but it meant nothing, just a reflexive lift of the sides of his mouth.

Dunc, on the other hand, was acutely aware of where he was and what was happening.

He looked around the darkened room, heard Melissa's even breathing, and saw her form in the shadows. He did not see the burglar, but he could see light from a nightlight in the hall coming through the partially opened door of Melissa's room, and he guessed that the burglar had gone into the hallway.

The house was silent.

Dunc started for the door, then realized Amos wasn't following him. He turned to see him apparently staring at Melissa.

"Come *on!*" he whispered, and grabbed Amos by the hand, jerked him out of the room and into the hallway. "You can stare at her later."

Amos followed happily, his feet trudging automatically.

It was just as well that Amos was unconscious. If he had known what was coming at him, there was a fair chance the shock would have come close to killing him.

In silence the boys entered the hallway. Dunc looked left and right, saw a glimmer of movement in a door to the right, and held out his hand to stop Amos. He put his mouth near Amos's ear and whispered softly, "You wait here. Guard Melissa, and I'll try to find the burglar. Got it?"

Amos smiled vacantly and moved his head in

what Dunc took to be a nod. Dunc moved off to the right down the hallway, while Amos stood near the door.

It was precisely then that a horrendous sound of cracking porcelain and splashing water came from the bathroom. The sound was barely over when the door across from Melissa's opened, and a huge frame filled the opening.

Rocko.

"What happens?" he said. His voice sounded like a speaker inside a steel barrel. "What happens bad?"

His eyes were like the ends of two rifle barrels, little holes of darkness swiveling to find whatever had caused the noise.

And he saw Amos.

Standing next to Melissa's door with an idiotic smile on his face.

It was still possible for Amos to have emerged safely, except that at the same instant that Rocko saw Amos, a small form came boiling out of the bathroom carrying a toilet on its shoulder. The burglar came out just as Dunc came in, knocking Dunc down and tripping him. Here timing became critically important.

Melissa's brother could have handled one

surprise fairly well, even one and a half, but two things happening at once confused Rocko.

And a confused Rocko was a bewildered Rocko.

And a bewildered Rocko instantly became an angered Rocko.

There was Amos standing by Melissa's door with a vacant smile on his face.

Trained by years of football and violence, Rocko grabbed the only weapon that was available to him and threw it at the burglar with the toilet.

He snaked one huge paw around Amos's neck, picked him cleanly up off the floor, and threw him at the burglar like a spear.

Amos spiraled once, lined up neatly on the target, and with the force of a bullet he jammed headfirst into the open end of the toilet on the burglar's shoulder.

The burglar stopped momentarily and tried to pull Amos out of the toilet. When he found that impossible, he changed the load so he could carry Amos more or less straight up and leaped through the open door to Melissa's room with both the toilet and Amos on his shoulder. All the noise had awakened Melissa just in time to see the burglar and Amos flying through her room toward the window.

Dunc dodged around Rocko and ran into Melissa's room just in time to see the burglar dive through the window, still carrying both the toilet and Amos, whose head was still jammed into the toilet.

"What . . .?" Melissa sat up in the bed.

Dunc paused with his hand on the window. "It's all right. This is all just a dream."

"Oh." Melissa nodded and lay back and closed her eyes just as Rocko barged into the room like an angry rhino. Dunc took one look at Rocko coming, saw death in his eyes, and dived full-length out the window. He landed on the ground just in time to see Amos disappearing into the hedges, his head still jammed in the toilet and the burglar carrying both of them easily.

"Don't worry, Amos!" Dunc yelled. "I'm coming!"

Which he meant to do, hoped to do, wanted to do—wanted to run and save his friend.

But he took one running step, and his foot came down on the same rake, lying in exactly the same place it had been lying for days, and the handle came up with the force of a bat, caught him vertically across the forehead, and seemed to make every streetlight in town light up in his brain. He went down like somebody dropping a bag full of sand.

"Amos—" he said, and then he said nothing.

Chapter · 11

The first thing Amos heard was the sound of gurgling.

A little water—or at least later he hoped it had been water, wished it had been water, convinced himself that it had been water—was still in the toilet and seemed to be sloshing around the top of his head.

He was moving.

For a moment that was all he could realize. He had been unconscious when everything had happened—had had no recollection of even going into Melissa's house, let alone encountering Rocko, the burglar, or the toilet. He remembered nothing that happened after the rake hit him.

He heard gurgling, and he was moving in some way he did not understand, and for a few minutes that was enough.

Then it came to him that it was dark. Not just dark from night, but *really* dark. He couldn't see anything.

Something was stuck on his head.

He tried to reach up and feel the object, but something else kept his arms pinned to his side. No, not something else—some*one* else.

Ah, yes, he thought. *I'm being carried by somebody. There is something jammed on my head, and I'm being carried by somebody. It all makes perfect sense.*

He fought to bring his memory back, but he could remember nothing after taking a step and the rake handle catching him.

All right, he thought. *Stick with what you know. I'm being carried by somebody, and there's something stuck on my head.*

Maybe it's Dunc.

"Dunc?" he said, or tried to say. The toilet made it impossible to form words correctly. It came out more like *gunk.* "Dunc?"

56

He heard the sound of an engine, and then he felt himself thrown into the back of a vehicle, headfirst, with whatever it was still stuck on his head.

"Oh, no, Carley—you've done it again."

It was a man's voice, low and even, as if the man were working to control being upset.

"This makes the fourth time in four months."

There was a sound without words, a kind of *ooooh-ooooh.*

I've heard that before, Amos thought. *I've heard that sound before. Somewhere—where? Ooooh-ooooh. Oh yes, now I remember.*

The zoo.

The monkey at the zoo. A chimp—what was her name? Kissing Gertie or something.

Again he catalogued what he knew. He was in the back of a vehicle that had started to move with something stuck on his head, and he wasn't alone—he was with a man and what might be a chimpanzee.

"I just wish you'd stick to your instructions a little less and think for yourself once in a while."

"Oooohhhh."

"I don't care how bad you feel. You were told to get the toilet."

"Oooohhh, ooohhh."

"I *know* you got the toilet, but you also got a little extra, didn't you?"

"Ooohhh."

"Yes. You grabbed a person *with* the toilet."

"Ooooooooo."

"You'd *better* be sorry. And you'd also better be thinking of what we're going to do with him."

Correction, Amos thought. *I'm sitting in a moving vehicle with a man and a monkey, and the man is talking to the monkey. Worse, he is asking the monkey for advice.*

It had to be the burglar.

This thought burned across his thinking. What else could it all have meant?

Correction number two, he thought. *I'm sitting in a vehicle with the burglar, who has somehow gotten a monkey to carry me away from Melissa's house with something stuck on my head even though he, the burglar, didn't want me, and he, the monkey, did want me.*

His brain flopped and stopped thinking.

Too much, he thought. *Too much thinking.*

He lay back and felt the vehicle turn a corner once, then again.

Amos reached up to feel the object on his head, to see how tight it was, to see if it could be removed. But as soon as he moved his arms, rough-textured hands grabbed his wrists and held them at his sides.

"Don't you hurt him, Carley—remember the last time and how messy it was when you hurt someone."

Amos felt the pressure lessen but remain firm.

He wiggled his eyebrows. Whatever had his head was cold, hard, and wet and jammed tightly, but he found that wiggling his eyebrows and forehead seemed to make the object pinch less.

He wiggled more.

It gave more, and he worked his eyebrows and forehead as hard as he could, and finally he felt his head come loose and move slightly out of the hole into which it was jammed.

The vehicle suddenly slowed, turned left, slowed still more, and stopped. The engine died.

"All right, Carley—you carried him in, you carry him out. And for Pete's sake, keep the toilet on his head. We don't want him to see anything."

Toilet? I'm stuck in a toilet?

The same coarse hands grabbed him by the sides and lifted him gently out of the vehicle, balanced the toilet on his head, and stood him on the ground, still holding his arms.

"Watch out," the man said to Amos. "We're going down the outside basement steps. Just move slowly."

How'd I get stuck in a toilet?

Chapter · 12

Amos felt the steps in front of his feet, and he let the monkey help him down. Then there was a short flat piece, two steps, and he heard a door open, and then four more steps, and the monkey stopped him.

"Winston, what in heaven's name are you doing with a boy with a toilet on his head?"

"I'm following your instructions, Mr. Waylon. I went to the library and found the message where you left it. You clearly said to steal a toilet from the same address as before."

"I most certainly did not."

"You did."

"I did not."

"Here's the note—read it."

There was a rustling sound of paper, then a snort from Mr. Waylon. "Clearly, Winston, this is not my handwriting."

"But—"

"Take him back."

"What?"

"Take the boy back, right now. *With* the toilet. And keep it on his head."

"But—"

"No *but*'s. You and Carley get him back to exactly the same place you found him, and you don't harm a hair on his head."

Amos had stood quietly all this time. He coughed now to clear his throat, the sound ringing inside the toilet. "Excuse me."

"What?" Mr. Waylon's voice snapped.

"Would you mind telling me what's going on?"

"Yes, I would mind. You don't need to know anything more than you already know."

"What am I going to tell them when I get back?"

"Tell them you were hijacked by a maniac who thought he had to steal toilets."

"What about the monkey?"

"You mean Carley? What about him?"

"How does he figure in all this?"

There was a long pause, and Winston finally sighed. "Why don't we tell him the truth? As long as he doesn't see us, what can he do?"

Another silence, then Mr. Waylon also sighed. "For once, I think you might be right. All right, listen—what's your name?"

"Amos."

"Listen, Amos. Waylon and Winston are not our real names. We used to work in a lab where they did experiments on cosmetics and medical problems. One day they brought in animals and started to use them for the experiments. One of the animals they brought in was Carley. Carley became a good friend and learned to play chess with us, and he would be a better friend except that he beats us all the time. So—"

Winston cut in. "So one day they came and said they wanted to use Carley for some of the testing and that it would injure Carley, and so we—well, kind of took Carley with us and left."

"But why do you go around stealing things?"

"We steal only luxury items from people who can afford to do without them."

"A toilet?"

"Well, that was a mistake. But we're going to return it."

Mr. Waylon interrupted. "We use the money to try to help animals around the world who are in the same position as Carley. Well, enough is enough, Winston. It's time to leave, Amos." Mr. Waylon grasped Amos's shoulder and turned him around, aiming him at the door. "Winston and Carley will take you back now. It was nice meeting you."

Winston and Carley guided Amos back up the steps and into the back of the van. The motor started, and the van moved, and it was in this way that half an hour later, Amos was found by a police officer wandering through the Hansens' backyard with a toilet on his head mumbling about monkeys and animals and saving Melissa.

"You there," the police officer called. "Hold it right there—I want to talk to you."

If Amos had done as the police officer had told him and held it right there, everything would have been all right.

But he didn't.

He turned toward the sound of the voice and reached up to take the toilet off his head and tell the police officer that he was a hero, that he was bringing back the toilet that had been stolen and that Melissa would probably wind up loving him for bringing the toilet back, or at least maybe like him a little or at the very least remember his name or even just learn his name.

But he got none of it out.

He took one step, just one, toward the police officer.

And stepped on the rake, which was lying exactly in the same position that it had been lying when he stepped on it the first time and the second time and when Dunc had stepped on it.

The rake, waiting like a cobra, waiting patiently in the darkness, came up. With the force of a runaway freight train it hit the toilet at exactly, perfectly the point it needed to drive it back into Amos's forehead. The blow shattered the toilet into a hundred pieces, ruining any chance Amos had of being a hero. But more important, it took away any remaining thoughts

65

Amos might have had and blew them into the ionosphere.

When he hit the ground, precisely one second after the blow, his brain was a blank space waiting to be signed.

Chapter · 13

"Wasn't it nice of them to put us in the same room?" Dunc was sitting on the edge of his bed in Clairview Memorial Hospital. They had been in overnight for observation, and the police had questioned them, or rather Dunc—Amos was still out—in the morning. Dunc had told the truth exactly as he knew it, and the police had believed him, or almost did—they remembered having run into Dunc and Amos before, when about half the town was blown up along the river and appliances were flying around like UFOs.

Amos shook his head. "Look, I know you and remember you—you're the one who got me into this. But I can't remember anything or anyone except my parents, who have grounded me until I'm drawing social security, and my sister, who calls me names that have *butt* in them."

He trailed off as a girl came into the room without knocking. She had blond hair and blue eyes and freckles, and Amos fought to keep the hospital gown closed in back.

The girl came to his bed, read his chart and looked up at him. "Are you Amos?"

Amos nodded.

She came around the side of the bed and reached over and hugged Amos. "I think you're very brave, and I want to thank you for saving me."

She turned and walked out.

Amos looked at the door. "Who was that?"

"That," Dunc said, smiling, "was Melissa."

"Who is Melissa?"

"Come on, you really don't know?"

Amos shook his head. "Some crazy girl comes in and hugs me, and I'm supposed to know her?"

"Melissa Hansen, Amos—that was *Melissa*."

Amos looked at the door to the room, struggled with his memories, and finally shrugged. "Doesn't ring a bell. She looks nice, but I've got

68

other problems. I keep having this dream or vision or something about a monkey driving a car and putting a toilet on my head—"

Dunc shook his head.

"—and it's so real. I mean, I can smell the toilet and feel the porcelain on my head. How can that be?"

Dunc looked out the window. Melissa was leaving the hospital. He watched her walking to where her parents were waiting in the parking lot two floors below, and he thought that when it finally came back, when Amos finally remembered, he was going to come apart.

"Monkeys and cars and men and driving and toilets—man, it's all so weird," Amos said.

I'll have to help him, Dunc thought. *I'm going to have to help him a lot when he comes out of this one.*

Be sure to join Dunc and Amos in these other Culpepper Adventures:

The Case of the Dirty Bird

When Dunc Culpepper and his best friend, Amos, first see the parrot in a pet store, they're not impressed—it's smelly, scruffy, and missing half its feathers. They're only slightly impressed when they learn that the parrot speaks four languages, has outlived ten of its owners, and is probably 150 years old. But when the bird starts mouthing off about buried treasure, Dunc and Amos get pretty excited —let the amateur sleuthing begin!

Dunc's Doll

Dunc and his accident-prone friend, Amos, are up to their old sleuthing habits once again. This time they're after a band of doll thieves! When a doll that once belonged to Charles Dickens's daughter is stolen from an exhibition at the local mall, the two boys put on their detective gear and do some serious snooping. Will a vicious watchdog keep them from retrieving the valuable missing doll?

Culpepper's Cannon

Dunc and Amos are researching the Civil War cannon that stands in the town square when they find a note inside telling them about a time portal. Entering it through the dressing room of La Petite, a women's clothing store, the boys find themselves in downtown Chatham on March 8, 1862—the day before the historic clash between the *Monitor* and the *Merrimac*. But the Confederate soldiers they meet mistake them for Yankee spies. Will they make it back to the future in one piece?

Dunc Gets Tweaked

Best friends Dunc and Amos meet up with Amos's cousin Lash when they enter the radical world of skateboard competition. When somebody "cops"—steals—Lash's prototype skateboard, the boys are determined to get it back. After all, Lash is about to shoot for a totally rad world's record! Along the way they learn a major lesson: *Never* kiss a monkey!

Dunc's Halloween

Dunc and his best friend, Amos, are planning the best route to get the most candy on Halloween. But their plans change when Amos is slightly bitten by a werewolf. He begins scratching himself and chasing UPS trucks: He's become a werepuppy!

Dunc Breaks the Record

Best-friends-for-life Dunc and Amos have a small problem when they try hang gliding—they crash in the wilderness. Luckily Amos has read a book about a boy who survived in the wilderness for fifty-four days. Too bad Amos doesn't have a hatchet. Things go from bad to worse when a wild man holds the boys captive. Can anything save them now?

Dunc and the Flaming Ghost

Dunc's not afraid of ghosts, but Amos is sure that the old Rambridge house is haunted by the ghost of Blackbeard the Pirate. Then the best friends meet Eddie, a meek man who claims to be impersonating Blackbeard's ghost in order to live in the house in peace. But if that's true, why are flames shooting from his mouth?